Samuel French Acting Edition

A Private Affair

by Charles Emery

‖SAMUEL FRENCH‖

SAMUELFRENCH.COM   **SAMUELFRENCH.CO.UK**

FOR PRODUCTION ENQUIRIES

UNITED STATES AND CANADA
Info@SamuelFrench.com
1-866-598-8449

UNITED KINGDOM AND EUROPE
Plays@SamuelFrench.co.uk
020-7255-4302

Each title is subject to availability from Samuel French, depending upon country of performance. Please be aware that *A PRIVATE AFFAIR* may not be licensed by Samuel French in your territory. Professional and amateur producers should contact the nearest Samuel French office or licensing partner to verify availability.

Please refer to page 38 for further copyright information.

A PRIVATE AFFAIR

STORY OF THE PLAY

The author of "The Glorified Brat" gives us a comedy contest-winner with riotous situations and sparkling characterizations. Poor Jefferson! All he wants is a quiet place to make his table lamps from absolutely empty liquor bottles. But the two women, one a psychiatrist, have not yet checked out of the hotel suite assigned to Jefferson through oversight. Seeing the empty bottles and lamp shades, the lady psychiatrist descends upon the innocent Jefferson, attempts to give him "the cure." She mistakes Jefferson for a man who had called on the phone and said he needed help because he "sees bulbs flashing." And when the woman from a temperance association shows up and sees all those empty bottles—that's the chip that causes an avalanche!

A PRIVATE AFFAIR

CHARACTERS
(As they appear)
(3 males; 4 females)

DORIS.............*secretary to a psychiatrist*

WOMAN.............*she with a problem child*

ELVIRA ....*the problem*

THEA.................*the lady psychiatrist*

JEFFERSON...*peace-loving man caught in a net*

BELLBOY...........*so very sure of everything*

THIN MAN.............*not sure of anything*

SETTING

The living room of a hotel suite.

TIME

About ten o'clock on a summer morning.

PRODUCTION NOTE: The purchase of cheap sun glasses with lenses carefully broken and removed from them can furnish Doris with a good pair of horn-rimmed glasses.

For

S.O. DOROTHY

A PRIVATE AFFAIR

DESCRIPTION OF CHARACTERS

DORIS: Is perhaps still in her twenties, a very efficient-appearing young woman. She wears horn-rimmed glasses and a plain tweed suit. It is possible that this part can be taken by an older woman, if desired, with no injury to the plot of the play.

THEA: Is an attractive, well-dressed young woman. Patience and gentleness combined with firmness are her foremost characteristics. Again it is possible that this part can be taken by an older woman, if desired, with no injury to the plot of the play.

ELVIRA: Perhaps around thirteen, though she may be younger. She is a genuine problem child; has ribboned pigtails.

WOMAN: Can be any age as long as she appears old enough to be Elvira's mother. Dresses rather sedately. She is demonstrative, opinionated and not a trifle smug, especially so in her last scene in the play.

JEFFERSON: A young man bewildered by a chain of events that surround him. Helplessly confused, innocent, and a victim of circumstance. He is neatly dressed. The part of Jefferson may also be played by an older man if desired, with no injury to the plot of the play.

BELLBOY: A young man, fresh-faced, sure of everything. He is dressed in a uniform.

THIN MAN: Skinny, nervous, confused; due to the fact he "sees bulbs flashing," he flutters his eyelids quite frequently. He can be any age. He is neatly dressed but wears a scotch plaid cap with its visor facing the back of his head.

6

A Private Affair

SCENE: *The living room of a hotel suite. Door Right leads to bedroom. Door Left leads to outside corridor. A folding screen at Rear Center supposedly hides a doorway to another room. Right Center, diagonally facing Left, is a large easy chair. Left Center, diagonally facing Right, is a divan. There is a small table bearing a telephone at the Right arm of the divan. Somewhere in the background are a couple of small chairs that can easily be lifted by women for a certain scene in the play. Other furniture may be added at the discretion of the director.*

TIME: *About ten o'clock on a summer morning.*

AT RISE: *No one is on stage. The audience sees only a closed suitcase standing in the middle of the floor and a woman's white slip spread upon the back of the easy chair. In a few seconds, DORIS enters. DORIS is perhaps still in her twenties, a very efficient appearing young woman. She wears horn-rimmed glasses and a plain tweed suit.*

DORIS. (*As she enters from bedroom.*) The suitcase is out here, Thea.

THEA. (*From off, bedroom.*) I knew it must be when we couldn't find it in here.

DORIS. (*Picks up suitcase and starts toward bedroom.*) It's after ten o'clock. Imagine, oversleeping like that. We were supposed to be out of here two hours ago.

THEA. (*From off, bedroom.*) I know it. We've missed the train. We'll have to stay over another day, that's all.

DORIS. (*Puts down suitcase, turns toward phone.*)

7

We're only paid up until eight o'clock this morning. I'd better call the desk and tell them we haven't checked out. (*Lifts phone from cradle.*)

THEA. (*From off, bedroom.*) We can do that later, Doris. Will you please bring in the suitcase? My face cream is in it.

DORIS. (*Replaces phone into cradle.*) We should have phoned the desk last night and asked them to call us this morning.

THEA. (*From off, bedroom.*) I thought I had the alarm all wound.

DORIS. You wound the alarm all right. The point is you forgot to set it. (*Picks up suitcase again.*)

THEA. (*From off, bedroom.*) Will you bring in the suitcase, please?

DORIS. (*Moving toward bedroom door.*) I'm coming with it. Whew, it's heavy. What's in it? An elephant? (*Goes off into bedroom.*)

(*There is a KNOCK on the door that leads to corridor.*)

THEA. (*From off, bedroom.*) See who's at the door, will you, Doris?

DORIS. (*Enters from bedroom.*) It's probably the hotel maid, wondering if we've gone. She's probably come to clean up the place.

(DORIS *opens the door leading to corridor. A middle-aged* WOMAN *stands there with a* LITTLE GIRL. *The* WOMAN *wears a hat with a feather curling from the front of it. The feather keeps bobbing over her forehead as she talks or moves. The* LITTLE GIRL *is thirteen and her hair is in ribboned pigtails. Both the* WOMAN *and* LITTLE GIRL *step inside as* DORIS *makes room for them to enter. The* CHILD'S *expression is positively disagreeable.*)

WOMAN. Oh, I guess I must have the wrong suite.

DORIS. For whom were you looking?

WOMAN. I'm looking for that lady psychiatrist who gave the lecture in town last night.

DORIS. (*Carefully.*) Was there something wrong with the lecture?

WOMAN. Oh, no. I heard very good reports about it. That's why I'm looking for the psychiatrist. The newspaper write-up said she was staying here.

DORIS. Do you have a problem?

WOMAN. I should say I *do* have a problem. It's Elvira here.

ELVIRA. (*Shouting.*) There's nothing wrong with me! There's nothing wrong with me!

WOMAN. (*Firmly.*) Oh, yes, there is, too.

THEA. (*From off, bedroom.*) Is that for me, Doris?

DORIS. (*Calling back to* THEA.) It's a woman and child who want to see the lady psychiatrist.

THEA. (*An attractive, well-dressed young woman; appears from bedroom.*) Well, ask them in.

ELVIRA. (*Noisily.*) I don't want to come in!

WOMAN. (*Scathingly.*) Sh! Of course you do. (*Tugs at* ELVIRA, *dragging her more fully into the room.*)

ELVIRA. (*Resisting heartily.*) I do not! I do not!

WOMAN. (*To* THEA, *with a loud sigh.*) She's a problem.

THEA. (*Smoothly.*) Oh, I'm sure she's not. (*To* ELVIRA.) You're not a problem, are you, dear?

ELVIRA. (*Emphatically.*) *She's* the problem.

WOMAN. Sh!

ELVIRA. Sh, yourself.

THEA. What seems to be the trouble?

WOMAN. Doughnuts. Cinnamon doughnuts. For months now all she'll eat for breakfast is cinnamon doughnuts. What kind of breakfast is that for a growing child?

THEA. Cinnamon doughnuts? (*Smiles sweetly at* ELVIRA.) Is that all you ever eat for breakfast?

ELVIRA. Wait'll *she* tells you what *she* has for breakfast every morning.

WOMAN. (*With dignity.*) She refers to my daily glass of goat's milk.

ELVIRA. (*Making a wry face.*) Ugh!

WOMAN. I try to explain to Elvira that goat's milk is all I need for breakfast but that *she's* a growing child.

ELVIRA. (*Mimicking.*) "She's a growing child!" Horsefeathers! I'm thirteen years old.

THEA. (*To* WOMAN.) Well, I wouldn't worry about the young lady too much.

ELVIRA. (*To* WOMAN.) See what she just called me? A young lady. It's time *you* realize it, too!

THEA. (*To* WOMAN.) Perhaps a few vitamin pills prescribed by your family doctor would be the answer.

ELVIRA. For Old Pale Face here, not for me. You ought to tell her to take some vitamins for what ails her head.

WOMAN. (*To* THEA.) Sass. Nothing but sass. You see the problem I have to contend with.

ELVIRA. (*Nodding in direction of* WOMAN.) And you see the problem *I* have to put up with, don't you? Nagging. Always nagging. From morning till night, nag, nag, nag.

THEA. (*To* WOMAN.) I wouldn't worry about her too much. Very young ladies often get a taste for one certain thing. They outgrow many little idiosyncracies.

WOMAN. Well, I don't want to take up your time. I know you must be a very busy person. But I felt I should consult you about Elvira. Do I owe you anything for the advice?

THEA. Not a thing. Glad if you can use it.

WOMAN. I *still* think she's a strange girl. Come along, Elvira. (*They exit by door leading to corridor.*)

DORIS. You certainly get some lulus in your profession.

THEA. The child seemed perfectly natural to me. A bit of the brat in her but quite normal.

ELVIRA. (*Opens corridor door, enters alone, quickly.*) I just came back to tell you. If you come up to see us sometime I'll share the loot with you.

THEA. Loot?

ELVIRA. Yeah. I got a *whole trunkful* of cinnamon doughnuts. (*Exits by door leading to corridor.*)

Doris. (*Smiling.*) Normal, huh?

Thea. Well, we psychiatrists aren't infallible, you know.

Doris. Thea, I've known you almost a year. For almost a year I've typed your records on patient after patient. It darned near has me convinced the whole world is nuts. I'm about ready to quit this job and go find me a good man and settle down.

Thea. Oh, one can do that anytime.

Doris. That's where you're wrong. Some day you're going to find you have nothing left but a file full of records. Then you'll wish you'd left this profession to some one else. Not that you aren't brilliant, mind you. But this is the quickest way I can imagine to end up in a booby hatch yourself.

Thea. Oh, I don't know. People stimulate me.

Doris. A bad wire plugged into an electric current can be stimulating, too. But who wants to be on the handling end of it?

Thea. We have to go in and straighten out the bedroom a little. Since we're staying here one more night, we'll try to use *this* room as little as possible.

Doris. Good idea. (*Moves toward phone.*) I'll call the desk and tell them we're staying over another day.

Thea. Before you do that will you come in and help me open that top bureau drawer? It's stuck again.

Doris. (*Turns toward* Thea.) Again?

Thea. (*As she and* Doris *move toward bedroom door.*) Yes. We may have to get the bellboy but let's try to get it open ourselves if we can. (*They disappear into bedroom.*)

(*There is the CLICK OF A KEY and the corridor door opens. A* Bellboy. *carrying two suitcases, enters with* Jefferson. Jefferson *is a conservatively dressed, serious-faced young man.*)

Bellboy. Here we are, sir.
Jefferson. Fine.

BELLBOY. (*Nodding toward bedroom door.*) Shall I take the suitcases into the bedroom, sir?

JEFFERSON. No. I can attend to those later. (*Points to the folding screen at Rear Center.*) What's that for?

BELLBOY. (*Sets suitcases at Left of divan.*) Oh, there's a little hallway behind that screen, sir. It's got no door so they keep the screen there. Beyond the hallway, behind the screen, there's another room.

JEFFERSON. (*Goes behind screen, comes back.*) That'll make a nice little workshop while I'm here.

BELLBOY. Yes, sir.

JEFFERSON. (*Passes* BELLBOY *tip.*) You can go now.

BELLBOY. Yes, sir. Thank you, sir. (*Exits by way of corridor door.*)

(JEFFERSON *picks up suitcases, starts toward screen; but the white slip on the back of the chair suddenly catches his eye. He sets down the suitcases, picks up slip, places it carefully across chair's back again. He goes to phone and lifts it from its cradle.*)

JEFFERSON. (*Into phone.*) Hello, desk? There's ah—ah, a woman's *underthing* left on the chair up here. (*After a pause, loudly.*) Of course I don't know whose it is! (*Slight pause, then.*) Will you please send up the boy to take it away? (*Replaces phone, picks up his two suitcases and disappears behind the screen.*)

DORIS. (*Enters from bedroom.*) Oh, it's out here, Thea. (*Takes slip from chair, goes slowly back toward bedroom.*)

THEA. (*From off, bedroom.*) I meant to put it in the suitcase we haven't finished packing. That slip was a present from an old patient of mine. A woman who used to think she saw dinosaurs every time she walked in the woods.

DORIS. Well, that's one good feature of being a doctor, anyhow. One gets a gift now and then. (*Exits to bedroom, slip on her arm.*)

(*There is a KNOCK on the corridor door.* JEFFERSON *appears from behind the screen, moving toward said door, and opens it.*)

BELLBOY. (*Entering.*) I came for the woman's underthing.

JEFFERSON. Oh, yes. It's on back of the chair there.

BELLBOY. Which chair, sir?

JEFFERSON. (*Points without looking.*) That chair.

BELLBOY. (*Goes to the chair indicated and looks carefully.*) I don't see any woman's underthing here, sir.

JEFFERSON. (*Still not looking at chair; a bit impatiently.*) Of course it's there. It's—what women wear.

BELLBOY. (*Examining chair thoroughly.*) You sure it isn't *wishful thinking,* sir?

JEFFERSON. (*Going toward chair.*) Oh, good heavens, can't you see— (*Stops short, surprised.*) Why, it's—it isn't there now.

BELLBOY. (*Looking at him sidewise.*) You were sure of it, sir?

JEFFERSON. Sure of it? Of course I was sure of it. I wouldn't have called the desk if I hadn't seen it.

BELLBOY. (*Scratches his head.*) I dunno. There's a lady down the hall that thinks there's a man in her closet every night. For five years she's called us every night. That's what we call *wishful thinking,* sir.

JEFFERSON. (*Somewhat muddled, reaches in pocket; hands* BELLBOY *a tip.*) Here, take this. Forget it.

BELLBOY. Certainly, sir. (*Winks at* JEFFERSON.) I know how you *feel,* sir.

JEFFERSON. (*Stiffly.*) That will be all.

BELLBOY. (*Smiling.*) Yes, sir. (*He still stands there, giggles a little.*)

JEFFERSON. (*Waving him away, annoyed.*) Well, goodbye.

BELLBOY. (*Nods.*) Goodbye, sir. (*Exits by corridor door.*)

(JEFFERSON *goes to chair where he had seen the slip;*

lifts cushion, replaces it; lifts chair back from floor a little; goes around chair, peering at it from the back. Finally he shakes his head, puzzled, and walks back toward screen, disappearing beyond it.)

THEA. (*Enters from bedroom.*) I'm going to call down and order a tray sent up. Coffee, toast and cereal. (*Calls back over her shoulder.*) How about you, Doris?

DORIS. (*From off, bedroom.*) Make it the same, please. I can do with a bite of breakfast.

THEA. (*Into phone.*) Hello, desk? Coffee, toast and oatmeal for two to be sent up to number thirteen, please. That's right. Thank you. (*Replaces phone in cradle.*)

DORIS. (*Enters from bedroom with the slip in her hand.*) Say, that's too bad.

THEA. What's too bad?

DORIS. Why, you must have caught this slip on the cover of your suitcase when you packed it. There's a tiny tear in it. I have a needle and thread here. I'm going to mend it for you.

THEA. Something is always catching on the lock of that suitcase. It's ruined about five pairs of nylons for me over the years.

DORIS. Cheaper to buy a new suitcase, I'd say. (*Sits in easy chair, starts to sew.*)

THEA. Do make a note of it. One new suitcase. I can't remember anything these days.

DORIS. I don't wonder, with the schedule you've made for yourself. From one town to another with these lectures nearly every night and the book you're writing in between times.

THEA. Perhaps if my book on psychiatry makes me a little money I can take a rest for a while.

DORIS. I'm having a wonderful time copying it on the typewriter for you. I especially liked the chapter about the man who kept an alligator in the bathtub.

THEA. Yes. That was just a misplaced desire to have something alive swimming near him. After psychiatry he was satisfied with two goldfish in a small bowl.

DORIS. (*Continuing to sew on the slip.*) It must give you a great deal of satisfaction to help people the way you have. Just the same I wish you'd learn how to relax more. There's a pack of playing cards in the bedroom. How about a game of cards?

THEA. Breakfast is on the way up.

DORIS. Well, we could *start* a game.

THEA. Well—all right.

DORIS. This was just a little tear. It's all fixed now. (*Breaks thread, lays slip across back of chair.*) Come on, let's start a game with the cards. (BOTH *exit to bedroom.*)

JEFFERSON. (*Enters from behind screen, goes to telephone; picks it up.*) Hello, desk. This is number thirteen. There's a big carton box that will be arriving for Jefferson Shelly. Will you send it up when it comes in? (*After a pause.*) That's right. I'm expecting it. Thank you. (*Cradles phone; starts back toward screen. But his eye catches the slip on the back of the chair, again. He does a double-take. Goes over and picks it up, letting it dangle between his hands.*) Now, see here. You *were* here and *are* here. What do you do? Walk away when I'm not looking? (*Places slip across back of chair, points to it accusingly.*) Now *this* time don't you go away. (*He makes a lunge for the phone, keeping his eyes on the slip.*) Hello, desk. There's—look, I *wasn't* seeing things. I mean— I mean there *is*—it's really so. (*After a pause.*) What am I trying to say? Why, just what I told you before! There's a woman's underthing on the back of this chair up here. (*After a pause.*) No, I don't know *who* it belongs to. But I want you to send up a boy to remove it. (*After a pause.*) No, no. To remove it from the *chair;* it's *not on anybody.* It's on the *chair.* (*After a pause.*) That's right. Hurry now before it goes away again! (*Hangs up, goes back to chair, pointing at the slip.*) Now, you stay right there *this* time. Don't you go away!

(*There is a KNOCK on the corridor door.* JEFFERSON

goes to answer. The BELLBOY, *tray containing two breakfasts in hand, enters briskly.*)

BELLBOY. Your breakfast, sir.

JEFFERSON. Breakfast? I didn't order anything. I never eat a breakfast.

BELLBOY. (*Placing tray on small table.*) Number thirteen, sir.

JEFFERSON. There's been a mistake. I didn't order any food. Now about the woman's underthing—the ah—the ah—*you* know.

BELLBOY. (*A loud sigh.*) Oh, sir, are we back to that again? Do we have to go back over all that? (*Faces* JEFFERSON, *trying to be firm.*) Now, look, sir. This is the way it is. You ordered *two* breakfasts from downstairs.

JEFFERSON. But I tell you I didn't.

BELLBOY. It's all right, sir. Hotel guests are allowed visitors as long as they don't disturb anybody. Perhaps you have a visitor here. Why should I care, sir? I'm interested only in my job. (*He moves toward corridor door,* JEFFERSON *moving determinedly after him.*)

JEFFERSON. (*Following* BELLBOY, *persistently.*) Young man, you didn't look on back of the chair this time! It *is* there again! It is, it is, it is!

BELLBOY. (*Goes out corridor door, hastily.*) Just call the desk when you're finished with the tray, sir.

(JEFFERSON *disappears, following* BELLBOY *out corridor door. While he is out,* DORIS *comes in from the bedroom and spies the waiting tray on the table.*)

DORIS. (*Calling out.*) Our breakfasts have arrived, Thea. I thought I heard some one come into the room out here. You'd have thought the bellboy would have had sense enough to knock on our bedroom door when he found the living room empty. (*She picks up the tray and starts toward bedroom door.*) It could have set there for hours and the coffee and cereal would have been stone cold. (*Spies the slip she left on chair back and picks it up with her free hand; exits to bedroom.*)

(JEFFERSON *returns from corridor door where he had tried to follow the* BELLBOY. *He is mopping his face with his handkerchief.*)

JEFFERSON. (*To no one, angrily.*) Nobody believes me, but, by jove, they're going to take that tray out of here and I'm not paying for it. Why should I pay for something I didn't order? (*Stops in his tracks.*) I thought that boy set that tray on this table. Why, it's *gone!* (*Swings around to look at chair where the slip was.*) And that thing is gone, too! Great Scott, it's walked away again! (*Mops his face with handkerchief.*) It *must* walk away. It keeps appearing and reappearing, vanishing and re-vanishing. Aspirin. I'm going to get me an aspirin. (*He goes off behind the screen.*)

(*The TELEPHONE rings.* THEA, *coffee cup in hand, comes out of bedroom to answer it.*)

THEA. (*Into phone.*) Hello? (*Pause.*) Yes, this is Doctor Thea Norton. (*Pause.*) Yes, I'm a psychiatrist. (*Pause.*) What's that? (*Pause.*) Well, I don't know. I only came into the city to lecture last night, not to solicit patients. What seems to be the trouble? (*Pause.*) I see. Well, all right. I can't give you more than a half hour, however. You see, I'm checking out tonight. (*Pause.*) Well, all right. But *only* a half hour. (*Pause.*) Yes, suite thirteen. (*Cradles phone.*)

DORIS. (*Enters from bedroom, coffee cup in hand.*) Who in heaven's name was that?

THEA. Some man in town called me. He's in the lobby now. He went to the lecture last night. He wants to see me about a problem.

DORIS. Don't they all! What's the problem?

THEA. He sees light bulbs.

DORIS. He sees *what?*

THEA. Light bulbs. They're in front of his eyes when there aren't any lights on. He can't sleep even when he puts out the lights because there are light bulbs flashing in droves in front of his eyes. Says it's the same in the daytime, too.

DORIS. Good heavens. I'd say he needed an electrician, not a psychiatrist.

THEA. Poor man. I hadn't the heart to tell him I couldn't see him.

DORIS. (*Sighs.*) No doubt. You know, I think we'll be lucky if we get out of this town and get on with the lectures. Everyone seems to be finding out where you're staying. And here we are, supposed to have checked out early this morning and I haven't even called the desk to tell the manager we haven't gone.

THEA. Well, we'll finish our breakfast in the other room first. It'll be cold if we don't. (*Places empty coffee cup on table.*) I'll say one thing, that coffee was good.

DORIS. Yes. That's more than can be said for some of the hotels we've stayed in on this tour. In some hotels all they do is boil the labels on the coffee cans. (*Places her cup on table.*)

THEA. Well, let's go back in there and finish the breakfast. (BOTH *exit to bedroom.*)

(*They have not left the room very long before there is a KNOCK on the corridor door. JEFFERSON comes from behind screen, goes to door and opens it. The BELLBOY stands there with a large carton box.*)

BELLBOY. (*Coming into room.*) Where do you want me to put it, sir? It's the box you phoned the desk about.

JEFFERSON. You can set it right down in the middle of the floor. I'm going to open it right away.

BELLBOY. (*Setting box in middle of floor.*) Plummet's Whisky, the label says. If there's as many bottles in there as I think there are—

JEFFERSON. Don't jump to conclusions, young man.

They're whisky bottles but they're empty. I use them to
make table lamps for people.

BELLBOY. (*Doubtfully.*) Well, if you say so.

JEFFERSON. It isn't just that I say so. It *is* so. That's
my business. I make table lamps from empty whisky
bottles and fancy lamp shades. I remove the labels from
the bottles and paint the bottles beautiful colors and
then I wire them up to make lamps.

BELLBOY. (*Shakes his head.*) If you say so, sir. It's
a relief from that other trouble you were giving me, anyhow. (*Suddenly remembering.*) If you're finished with
your tray now, I'll take it down with me.

JEFFERSON. Tray? What tray? (*He suddenly under-
stands.*) Oh, you mean that breakfast tray.

BELLBOY. Precisely, sir.

JEFFERSON. Well, I don't know where it went. When
I came back from chasing you in the corridor it was gone.

BELLBOY. (*Lifting his eyebrows.*) Gone, sir?

JEFFERSON. Yes. So was the you-know-what.

BELLBOY. Look, I'm not going back over all that.
When the dame is finished eating, just buzz the desk. I'll
come up and get the tray.

JEFFERSON. Dame? What dame?

BELLBOY. Aw, mister, I told you it was all right.
You're allowed visitors. Why be so secretive?

JEFFERSON. Secretive? Why should I be secretive when
I don't even know what you're talking about?

BELLBOY. The desk told me it was a woman who put
the call in for the breakfast in number thirteen, sir. So
even the desk isn't angry. See? They *know* you have a
woman up here.

JEFFERSON. There are no women here. I'm alone. Absolutely alone.

(*There is a KNOCK on the corridor door.* BELLBOY *and*
JEFFERSON *look at each other for a short moment.*)

BELLBOY. Ha! Bet that's the dame! (*Wags a finger
at* JEFFERSON.)

JEFFERSON. (*Goes to door and opens it.*) Come in.

(*A thin man wearing a scotch plaid cap enters the room. The visor of the cap faces the back of his head.*)

THIN MAN. (*Entering.*) Where is she?

JEFFERSON. Where is who?

THIN MAN. The woman who's expecting me.

BELLBOY. Ha! I *knew* it. (*To* JEFFERSON.) See? Here's a man who knows you have a woman hidden here somewhere.

THIN MAN. (*To* JEFFERSON.) There's no reason to hide her. She knew I was coming. I called her on the phone.

JEFFERSON. I've no idea what you're talking about, my good man. No idea whatever. It's quite possible you have the wrong suite.

THIN MAN. Isn't this suite number thirteen?

JEFFERSON. Yes.

THIN MAN. Then it must be *you're* in the wrong suite. Suite thirteen is the number the woman gave me. I'm expected. I'm the man who sees light bulbs.

JEFFERSON. You mean you're from the electric light power company?

THIN MAN. No. I'm the man who sees light bulbs. I see light bulbs when I walk down a street and there aren't any there. I see light bulbs when all the lights are out and I try to sleep at night. All the time I see light bulbs when there *aren't* any light bulbs to be seen.

JEFFERSON. What you need is a psychiatrist.

THIN MAN. That's just why I called on the phone. And *this* was the place she said to come.

BELLBOY. (*Shakes his head, despairingly.*) I give up. (*To the* THIN MAN.) *This* one (*Indicates* JEFFERSON *with a pointing thumb*) is always seeing some woman's underthing on the back of a chair when there *isn't* any underthing to be seen.

THIN MAN. (*To* JEFFERSON, *relieved.*) Oh, now I understand. *You've* come to see the woman doctor, too. Isn't it awful the way some of us are seeing things that aren't there these days? The world must be full of people like us.

BELLBOY. (*Dryly.*) One makes lamps and the other sees bulbs. (*Sighs loudly.*) You say the world is full of people like you. If it is, I don't see why you all have to come to *this* hotel. There's five other hotels in town. (*To* JEFFERSON.) I know you'll find the breakfast tray I sent up. Not that *I* care, but the hotel trusts its guests.

JEFFERSON. (*Holds out a coin to* BELLBOY.) Here.

BELLBOY. No. I won't take your money. Not because I don't need it, but because I don't want people questioning me later in case you don't remember you offered it to me.

JEFFERSON. My memory is excellent.

BELLBOY. I hope you'll remember what you did with the tray, then, sir. (*He exits corridor door.*)

THIN MAN. So you make lamps.

JEFFERSON. Yes. Out of empty whisky bottles. The bellboy doesn't believe me but I can prove it. (*He goes to carton box in middle of floor; takes a knife from his pocket, breaks the string, and opens it. He tips box upside gently and out rolls many empty liquor bottles along with fancy lamp shades with ribbons, etc.*)

THIN MAN. (*Bewildered.*) I don't see any bottles.

JEFFERSON. (*Surprised.*) You don't?

THIN MAN. (*Gasps.*) No. (*His voice trembles.*) I can't see anything but bulbs flashing. (*Moans.*) It's starting up again, my trouble. (*Stares fixedly at closed bedroom door.*) There's a red bulb flashing off and on over there by that door. I never got a *red* bulb before. (*Tremulously.*) Up till now they've all been ordinary bulbs.

JEFFERSON. (*Picks lamp shade with ribbons from floor, puts it on his own head.*) Can't you see this? It's a lamp shade. I've put it on my head.

THIN MAN. No. I can't see a thing but bulbs flashing. How long will it be before the woman doctor shows up?

JEFFERSON. What woman doctor? There's no one here but me. I'm absolutely alone here.

THIN MAN. I must have misunderstood the suite number but I was sure she said number thirteen. (*Moves toward corridor door.*) I'll have to inquire at the desk. (*He staggers a little due to his condition.*) I hope I can find my way to the elevator. (*Exits corridor door.*)

THEA. (*Enters from bedroom; sees JEFFERSON for the first time.*) Oh, I'm sorry to have kept you waiting. (*Obviously she thinks he is the patient that phoned her.*) I didn't hear you knock.

JEFFERSON. (*Lamp shade with big bow ribbons still on his head.*) Where—where did you come from?

THEA. You couldn't have knocked very loudly.

JEFFERSON. But I didn't know you were in that other room!

THEA. You poor man. I remember you said you saw light bulbs. But I didn't think it had gone to the extent where you wear a lamp shade on your head.

JEFFERSON. (*Trying to explain.*) But I was just showing—

THEA. (*Interrupting.*) Now first I'll have to ask you a few questions. When did you begin to have the hallucinations about the light bulbs?

JEFFERSON. (*Still trying to explain.*) But it wasn't—I wasn't the one who saw the bulbs flashing. It—it was that thin man who was just here.

THEA. Now, don't get panicky. Why don't you sit down right here where we can talk. (*Leads him to easy chair and seats him.*) This is all very interesting. You say you also saw a thin man. What was he doing?

JEFFERSON. It was the thin man who was just here. He, not I, saw bulbs flashing. I am not he. He is not me. I mean—

THEA. (*Calling out.*) Doris, would you come here for a moment?

DORIS. (*Appears from bedroom.*) I'm right here, Thea.

THEA. (*A loud whisper.*) Stay by the phone. He *might* be dangerous.

DORIS. (*Hissing back a whisper.*) Right!

THEA. (*Circling around chair, standing in back of* JEFFERSON.) Now, why don't you just close your eyes for a minute. That way you can relax and perhaps I can help you.

JEFFERSON. (*Closes his eyes briefly, then opens them widely, pointing at* DORIS.) And where did *that* one come from?

THEA. That's my secretary. She's been here right along.

JEFFERSON. She has? There's some mistake—

THEA. Now about this thin man you say you saw. Do you see him often? When you see bulbs flashing do you also see him?

JEFFERSON. No. I mean I *did* see him. He was here. But I was—it is *not* I who sees bulbs flashing. It was the thin man who came in and then went out.

THEA. (*To* DORIS.) Schizophrenia. Split personality. Sometimes thinks he's somebody else.

JEFFERSON. (*Makes a move to rise from chair.*) But I tell you—

THEA. (*Hastily.*) No, no. Don't get up. Stay near the phone, Doris.

JEFFERSON. Why should she stay near the phone? You make it sound as if I might be dangerous. I am not dangerous.

THEA. (*Soothingly.*) Of course you're not dangerous. We just thought the phone might ring. If it does and I'm busy with you, then there has to be somebody to answer the telephone, doesn't there?

DORIS. (*Points to floor, gasping.*) Oh, good heavens, look!

THEA. (*Moves from* JEFFERSON'S *chair to middle of floor.*) Liquor bottles! Ten bottles of Plummet's Whisky! Good grief, no wonder the man sees bulbs flashing! He's drunk.

JEFFERSON. I heard what you said. It just isn't so.

DORIS. After drinking all that it's a wonder he can see anything.

THEA. And lamp shades! There are ten lamp shades among them.

DORIS. He must have been going around to the different suites, stealing the shades off lamps. Hadn't I better call the desk?

THEA. No. Not yet anyway. This man really needs help.

JEFFERSON. (*Groaning.*) You've got everything all wrong. Things aren't at all as you see them. It's tricks that appearance you. I mean it's appearances that trick you. I had ordered those bottles to—

THEA. (*Interrupting.*) I just don't see how you could have drunk all that liquor in that short time. Maybe one bottle, perhaps two, yes. But *not* all ten of them! How long had you been out here drinking before we saw you?

JEFFERSON. If only you'd let me explain. I do *not* drink. I do *not* see bulbs flashing. I wire bottles to bulbs—

THEA. (*To* DORIS.) Poor man. (*To* JEFFERSON.) I'm afraid I can't help people who have been drinking too much.

JEFFERSON. (*Rising, loudly.*) But I'm sober! I am, I am!

THEA. (*Gently.*) Now, sit down, and listen carefully to what I recommend.

JEFFERSON. But why should I listen when I know more about me than you do?

THEA. (*Coldly.*) If you feel this way, then why did you phone me to come here in the first place?

DORIS. (*Wearily.*) Why not let me call the desk and have them come up and take him away?

THEA. No, that won't settle anything. I'd have it on my conscience that I didn't try to help. There's a reason why people drink. The idea is to get to the bottom of it.

JEFFERSON. This is *my* suite. What are you doing in *my* suite?

DORIS. (*Shakes her head.*) He certainly is tanked up. Now he thinks he *lives* here.

THEA. I'm afraid I can't get him to listen to me in his

condition. Perhaps if he can lie down awhile and sleep it off, then I could talk with him.

DORIS. I wouldn't risk a professional reputation such as you have. What if the bellboy or some one in the hotel got wind of the fact we're hiding a man up here?

THEA. But we're *not hiding* a man. We're trying to *help* a man.

DORIS. I know. But the appearance of things—

JEFFERSON. If you two have come here to rob me why don't you just take my wallet and leave? There's fifty dollars in it. Take it if you want it. All I ask is to let me alone with my bottles and my lamp shades. I have a lot of wiring to do—

DORIS. Now he thinks we want to rob him!

THEA. Only because of his condition. He could see we're decent people if he were sober.

JEFFERSON. I repeat, I *am* sober! I'm as sober as your grandfather taking your grandmother to church.

THEA. (*Pointing to screen.*) There's a little room behind that screen.

JEFFERSON. I *know* there's a little room there. That's where I've been spending my time.

DORIS. Oh, dear. You don't suppose there are more whiskey bottles and lamp shades *in there,* do you?

THEA. (*To* JEFFERSON.) If my secretary and I help you to that screen, will you go into that little room and lie down?

JEFFERSON. I am perfectly able to walk to that little room by myself. Why should either of you help me? And why should I lie down? I feel perfectly all right except—

THEA. Come, Doris, help me with him. We mustn't let him fall. He might try to sue us later.

(THEA *and* DORIS *come to each side of him, pulling him gently toward the screen, appearing to lend him support.*)

DORIS. Isn't it amazing? All those bottles and he's walking perfectly straight.

THEA. (*As they draw him gently toward screen.*) Now you're to lie down for at least an hour. You're to try to sleep.

JEFFERSON. Sleep? But why should I sleep? I don't feel sleepy. *I am not sleepy.*

THEA. (*As to pacify.*) And then later—when you come out—I'll listen to everything you have to say.

JEFFERSON. (*Having reached screen, turns to face the* WOMEN.) Is that the only way I can get you to listen to me?

THEA. That's the only way.

JEFFERSON. All right, ladies. You win. I'll go in there. I don't promise to sleep but I'll go in. And when I come out again you've promised you'll listen to me.

THEA. Of course.

JEFFERSON. And you'll let me talk without interrupting me?

THEA. Naturally.

JEFFERSON. You know, ladies, this is the first time I've ever been invaded in a hotel suite paid for in advance. I've lived in hotels all my life and never has anyone— man or woman—invaded my privacy. I should call the desk and report you for entering without cause. The reason I don't do that is because there's been a mix-up of some kind and I don't think it's your fault.

THEA. (*Soothingly.*) There, there. You'll feel better in a little while. Then we'll talk.

JEFFERSON. You promised then *I* could talk.

THEA. Certainly. After you've rested.

JEFFERSON. I'll have no rest till I *have* talked. (*Exits behind screen.*)

DORIS. (*Moving toward phone.*) I think I'll call the desk.

THEA. (*Moving toward her quickly.*) What for?

DORIS. To have them come up and remove him. I'm not going to have you risk your reputation on an insane episode like this. That man has gulped down all that liquor and collected lamp shades out of ten hotel suites.

He might be dangerous. He might even be carrying a gun.

THEA. (*Draws* DORIS *gently from phone.*) Think of it this way, Doris. My reputation can be just as soiled if the people at the desk know there's a drunk up here, no matter what story *we* tell. It *still* wouldn't look good. Whereas, this other way, he rests, he talks, and he leaves and maybe I've helped him.

(*There is a KNOCK on the corridor door.*)

DORIS. Now what?
THEA. Answer it.

(DORIS *goes to corridor door, opens it.* BELLBOY *steps inside.*)

BELLBOY. Ha! I knew it! I knew it all the time!
THEA. Knew *what* all the time?
BELLBOY. I knew there was a couple of babes in this place.
DORIS. We're guests and we're ladies. We are *not* babes.
BELLBOY. Well, the desk has insisted I bring back the tray. The hotel is short on trays. Do I get it, or don't I?
THEA. Of course. It's in the other room. Doris, get the breakfast tray, will you? (DORIS *exits to bedroom.*)
BELLBOY. Then you *admit* there *was* a tray.
THEA. Admit it? Why, we never denied it.
BELLBOY. Now we're cooking with gas.
THEA. I beg your pardon?
DORIS. (*Re-enters from bedroom with tray.*) Here you are, Fresh Boy.
BELLBOY. (*Taking tray; making a mock bow.*) Thank you, madame. (*Exits corridor.*)
DORIS. (*To* THEA.) Do you think he knows there's a man here?
THEA. What difference does it make? We've done nothing wrong.

DORIS. I'll be glad when this town is behind us. Remind me to cancel it from your next lecture tour.

THEA. Doris, do you realize we haven't yet called the desk, telling them we didn't check out this morning?

DORIS. I've started to call them several times. Something's always come up.

THEA. First thing you know they'll think we left early this morning and they'll be assigning the suite to somebody else.

DORIS. I know. That would put us in an awkward position, wouldn't it?

THEA. First would you mind picking up those lamp shades and bottles and taking them into the bedroom? If anyone else comes in they'll see them out here.

DORIS. (*Gathering up the lamp shades.*) What do you suppose he was going to do with all these? Sell them to people?

THEA. It's difficult to tell.

DORIS. (*Going toward bedroom, arms full of shades.*) I'll be back for the bottles in a minute. (*Exits to bedroom.*)

(*There is a KNOCK at the corridor door. THEA goes to answer. The WOMAN has returned, but she is without ELVIRA.*)

WOMAN. May I come in?

THEA. Yes, of course.

WOMAN. (*Entering fully into room.*) I'm almost beside myself.

THEA. Really? What seems to be the trouble?

WOMAN. Why, I've *lost* Elvira. We left here and then went into a grocery store to do some shopping and when I turned around she was gone!

THEA. The little girl who liked cinnamon doughnuts?

WOMAN. Yes. And that's not the worst of it. At the same time I missed Elvira the woman clerk was yelling to the manager that seven boxes of cinnamon doughnuts were missing. You can imagine how I felt! All those doughnuts and Elvira missing at the *same* time.

THEA. Well, it might be that she didn't take them, you know. Things are not always what they appear to be.

WOMAN. Oh, I'll pay for the doughnuts if she took them. But I *can't* find *her*. That's what worries me. I thought she might have come back here.

THEA. No. She isn't here.

WOMAN. (*Pointing to screen.*) You don't suppose she sneaked back somehow and is hiding behind that?

THEA. I'm sure she isn't here.

WOMAN. May I look behind there and see? Just to make sure?

THEA. (*Uncomfortably.*) I'd rather you wouldn't.

WOMAN. Well, then, would *you* look?

THEA. (*Moving toward screen.*) Yes, certainly. (*She disappears behind the screen.*)

DORIS. (*As she comes out of bedroom.*) And *now* for the empty whisky bottles. (*Stops short as she sees* WOMAN.)

WOMAN. (*Turning her gaze upon the group of bottles on floor.*) Well! That's quite a lot of liquor, I'd say, for *even two* women to have been drinking.

DORIS. (*Helplessly.*) Thea!

THEA. (*Reappearing from behind screen.*) No. She's not in there.

WOMAN. (*With severity.*) I *hope* you were *able* to *see* whether she was or not.

THEA. Madame?

WOMAN. (*Archly.*) I was just telling your friend here that it's beyond my comprehension how two women could consume all that liquor.

THEA. (*Laughing.*) They're only empty bottles.

WOMAN. (*Suspiciously.*) I see they are. Empty *now*.

DORIS. (*Scooping up bottles, nervously dropping some of them.*) You explain to her, Thea. (DORIS *goes off to bedroom with six of the bottles.*)

THEA. (*To* WOMAN.) You see, some one brought them in here when we weren't looking.

WOMAN. It's none of my business, of course. But I don't see any left with the liquor still in them. Does the medical profession condone liquor?

THEA. I'm a psychiatrist, not a medical doctor, but I certainly don't recommend drinking.

WOMAN. (*Sniffs.*) Then why do you do it? I certainly wouldn't have brought Elvira here in the first place if I'd known you were a drinking woman.

THEA. You misunderstand—

WOMAN. Things are pretty clear, I'd say. I felt from the beginning you were much too easy on Elvira. Apparently you're one of these *modern* women who believe in this *progressiveness* that some people speak of.

THEA. (*With dignity.*) I charged you nothing for the advice I gave on Elvira.

WOMAN. (*Crisply.*) I'm beginning to see now why you didn't.

THEA. (*As* DORIS *comes back for more bottles.*) What do you mean by that?

WOMAN. (*Counting bottles quickly as* DORIS *hurries by her with four more.*) One, two, three, four more. Added to the six she took in before, that makes *ten* bottles. *Ten bottles!*

THEA. You shouldn't judge by appearances.

WOMAN. What else is there to judge by? I didn't see a *milk* bottle among them. (*Her tone would freeze an Eskimo.*) Young woman, I'm a member in good standing of an upright organization known as the W.A.A.A. That stands for Women's Association Against Alcohol. We know liquor to be half the trouble with our world today. (*Raises her fist and shakes it in the air.*) And we intend to fight against this scalding fire in these wicked bottles with every last ounce of blood that's in us!

THEA. I certainly don't approve of anything without moderation.

WOMAN. And yet ten bottles I counted! Ten of them! Ten bottles of hell fire and damnation consumed by two women in a hotel suite in a town that's been dry since prohibition!

THEA. I've been trying to tell you that—

WOMAN. (*Over-riding* THEA.) You come here from the city and are supposed to be a brilliant woman. You give a fine lecture on how psychiatry cures the mind. People listen to you and applaud you and write you up prettily in the newspapers. And then (*Points to floor where bottles were*) this!

THEA. Madame, I have a patient on the way up. I shall have to ask you to leave.

WOMAN. (*After a quick pause.*) Very well, I shall leave. But I shall see to it that you are not welcome in this town again. The Women's Association Against Alcohol will attend to *that*.

THEA. (*Going toward bedroom.*) Good day, madame. (*Exits bedroom.*)

(*The* WOMAN *starts to leave by door leading to corridor, but at this moment* JEFFERSON *comes out from behind the screen.*)

JEFFERSON. Oh, I beg your pardon.

WOMAN. (*Pauses in her tracks; turns around slowly; speaks smugly.*) So—they're *entertaining a man* in secret, too! The desk downstairs will hear about this!

JEFFERSON. For whom were you looking? This is *my* suite.

WOMAN. (*Indignantly.*) A likely story! I can see now why those women didn't want *me* to look behind the screen for Elvira.

JEFFERSON. I came out because I am not sleepy.

WOMAN. I shouldn't think so after wallowing in all that liquor!

JEFFERSON. I've tried to explain to people I do not drink. I wire bottles to bulbs—

WOMAN. No doubt you've had enough to swing from a chandelier. People who drink are apt to try *anything*.

JEFFERSON. Pardon me, I just remembered. I think I've left a cigarette burning in the other room. (*He goes back behind screen.*)

WOMAN. (*Raising her voice to the vanished* JEFFERSON.) I'll also have you know that the Women's Association Against Alcohol is also against the evils of poisonous tobacco!

THIN MAN. (*Entering from corridor door after a quick knock.*) Ah, here you are. I can see a portion of you.

WOMAN. (*Swings her attention to* THIN MAN.) So there were *two* men all the time! Two men carousing with two women, swallowed up in the evils of alcohol and tobacco!

THIN MAN. You must have me mixed up with some one else, Doctor. I'm the man who called you downstairs awhile ago. I'm the man who sees light bulbs.

WOMAN. I am not a doc—

THIN MAN. (*Grabs her strongly.*) Doctor, I need help! A man here a while ago said there was no woman doctor here, but I can see the outline of a woman and you have a woman's voice.

WOMAN. (*Trying to wrench free.*) Unhand me, sir! Remove your grip from me this instant!

THIN MAN. It's only that I can't see you completely. If I don't hang on I'm apt to fall. Hold me! Hold me tight!

WOMAN. (*Furiously, freeing herself.*) I shall *not* support an imbiber!

THIN MAN. (*Desperately.*) You must help me! You must! You're just one big purple bulb that keeps flashing!

WOMAN. (*Screaming loudly.*) Help! Send help! Suite thirteen! *Send help!*

THIN MAN. (*Mystified.*) But I *told* you I was coming.

WOMAN. (*Eludes him, running out of door leading to corridor.*) Help! Help! *Send help! Suite thirteen!*

(THIN MAN *chases out after her and CONTINUED SCREAMS are heard in the distance.*)

THEA. (*Entering from bedroom,* DORIS *behind her.*)

Good heavens! (*As* Doris *goes toward screen.*) He has some woman in there.

Doris. It sounds as if he's killing her!

Jefferson. (*Appearing from behind screen; he speaks of the cigarette he went to extinguish.*) I left one burning all right. I killed it.

Thea. (*Gasps.*) Oh, no! Doris, call the desk. This man is psychopathic!

Doris. (*Dashing for phone.*) Pick up that chair there, Thea, and ward him off till I can get help.

Thea. (*Picks up small chair, holds it above* Jefferson's *head.*) You stay right where you are. You stay (Jefferson *makes an abrupt move, she also*) right where you are.

Jefferson. Ladies, don't you think this nonsense has gone far enough? Won't you please go and leave me in peace? (*He keeps dodging and* Thea *keeps dodging to cover him with chair.*)

Doris. (*Into phone.*) Hello, desk—there's a man up here who has just killed a woman. (*Pause.*) Yes, and he says he's left her burning. (*Pause.*) Yes, in the room behind that screen. Please hurry! (*Bangs down phone, rushes to another small chair, picks it up. Both women guard him with chairs from each side.*)

Thea. Remain calm, Doris. The thing to do is to remain calm.

Doris. (*Stuttering.*) I—I am—*am* c-calm.

Jefferson. (*Bewildered.*) I am not sleepy. Why should you wish to bang me over the head because I'm not sleepy?

Thea. (*To* Doris.) Are they sending some one up?

Doris. Yes. Right away.

Jefferson. (*To* Doris.) I heard you when you were on the phone. I never killed anyone in my life.

Thea. Doris, he said he left her burning. You'd better go see. The whole hotel will be in flames.

Doris. Are you sure you can guard him all alone?

Thea. Yes, yes. Go see.

(Small chair still in her hand, DORIS disappears behind screen.)

JEFFERSON. *(To THEA.)* You are two ridiculous women who have invaded the privacy of my suite. Now you're trying to snare me by telling lies about me to the downstairs desk.

THEA. You said yourself you—

DORIS. *(Comes out from behind screen.)* Why, there's nothing. Nobody's in there.

THEA. No one at all?

DORIS. Why, no.

THEA. You'd better help me keep him covered. If he has such hallucinations he's *still* dangerous.

JEFFERSON. *(Reaches in pocket, pulls out billfold; throws it in direction opposite to corridor door.)* There it is—fifty dollars. Please take it and go now.

THEA. Doris, pick up his wallet. *(DORIS goes toward billfold to retrieve it.)* We don't want your money.

JEFFERSON. *(Points to corridor door.)* I'm going out of here so clear the way.

THEA. *(Makes a quick move to cover him with chair.)* You're not—

(JEFFERSON pretends to move to Right but suddenly moves to Left, outsmarts her. He dashes toward corridor door and exits.)

DORIS. *(Having retrieved billfold, gasps.)* You let him get away!

THEA. I *didn't* let him. He *tricked* me!

DORIS. Now the whole hotel is in danger. There's a madman on the loose.

THEA. Call the desk again, Doris. Have them stop him on the way out of the lobby. Describe him to them. Dark gray suit, thick brown hair, with a little mole under his left eye—

(DORIS rushes to phone but before she reaches it, BELL-BOY enters from corridor door after a quick knock.)

BELLBOY. Well, where is he?

THEA. } (*Together.*) {We—he got away.
DORIS. } {He tricked us!

BELLBOY. (*Goes toward screen.*) There'd really better be a dead woman behind here just as you told the desk. Because, if there *isn't*, the hotel is going to bounce you right out into the street. (*Disappears behind the screen.*)

THEA. (*To* DORIS.) Bounce us into the street? Why, they can't do that.

DORIS. I should say not. We ordered and paid for this suite. (*Covers her mouth quickly, then gasps, remembering.*) We didn't phone them downstairs that we were staying over today. We're only paid up to eight o'clock this morning.

THEA. (*With a sigh.*) Is there *anything* we *did* do right?

BELLBOY. (*Reappearing from behind screen.*) Just as I figured. Nobody there. It's just a case of wanting to keep the hotel all stirred up. (*To* THEA *and* DORIS.) You've given us enough trouble this morning. You've had the whole hotel in an uproar with all that screaming up here.

THEA. We didn't scream.

DORIS. We haven't made a sound.

THEA. We *heard* a scream. We thought—

BELLBOY. Yeah? (*To* DORIS.) And what are *you* doing with a man's billfold in your hand?

DORIS. (*Suddenly aware, looking at billfold.*) Why, I—

THEA. The man that was here threw it at us and insisted we keep it.

BELLBOY. Yeah? That doesn't ring a bell with me. Every hotel knows the kind of women who get a man drunk, rob him, and then scream that he's harming them. You two better come downstairs with me.

THEA. This is ridiculous!

DORIS. Absurd!

BELLBOY. There's nothing amusing about it to the desk. They've already called the cops. You can come with me quietly and save face. Or you can wait till the cops come up here and ride down the elevator with them. Take your pick.

THEA. But you don't understand—

DORIS. Of course he doesn't! That man was here—

BELLBOY. Which will it be—on the elevator with me or with the cops while everybody on the elevator stares at you?

THEA. But we're not packed up yet.

DORIS. Of course not. We can't leave all our things in that other room.

BELLBOY. The hotel will pack them up for you. They'll be sent to any address you give if you leave money to forward them. But where you're both going I don't think you'll be needing them for a while.

THEA. This is preposterous!

DORIS. It's outrageous. Absolutely outrageous!

BELLBOY. (*Gesturing with his thumb toward corridor door.*) Yeah, I know. Let's go.

(THEA *and* DORIS *march out ahead of him and he follows, the door closing behind him. There is a slight pause, the room now completely empty of people. Then the corridor door opens softly, slowly, and* ELVIRA *enters. Her arms are loaded with packages of cinnamon doughnuts. Cautiously, she goes to peek behind the screen. She then tiptoes toward bedroom door, peeking beyond. Finally she goes to the easy chair and sits. She arranges the boxes in stacks on her lap, opening one of them. She makes loud rustling noises with the inside waxed paper.*)

ELVIRA. (*Biting into a doughnut.*) I guess I'll have to eat 'em all myself. I wonder where the two nice ladies went.

CURTAIN

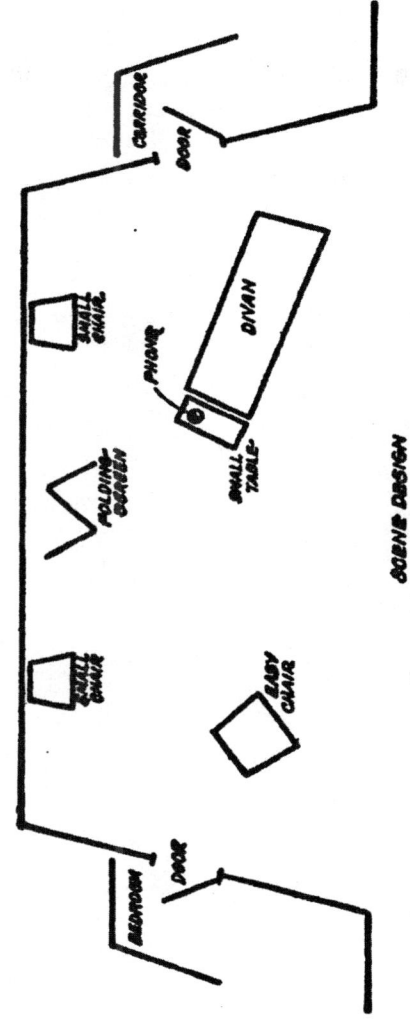

SCENE DESIGN
"A PRIVATE AFFAIR"

MUSIC USE NOTE

Licensees are solely responsible for obtaining formal written permission from copyright owners to use copyrighted music in the performance of this play and are strongly cautioned to do so. If no such permission is obtained by the licensee, then the licensee must use only original music that the licensee owns and controls. Licensees are solely responsible and liable for all music clearances and shall indemnify the copyright owners of the play(s) and their licensing agent, Samuel French, against any costs, expenses, losses and liabilities arising from the use of music by licensees. Please contact the appropriate music licensing authority in your territory for the rights to any incidental music.

IMPORTANT BILLING AND CREDIT REQUIREMENTS

If you have obtained performance rights to this title, please refer to your licensing agreement for important billing and credit requirements.